STEP INTO READING STEP 1

DC SUPER FRIENDS™

FLYING HIGH

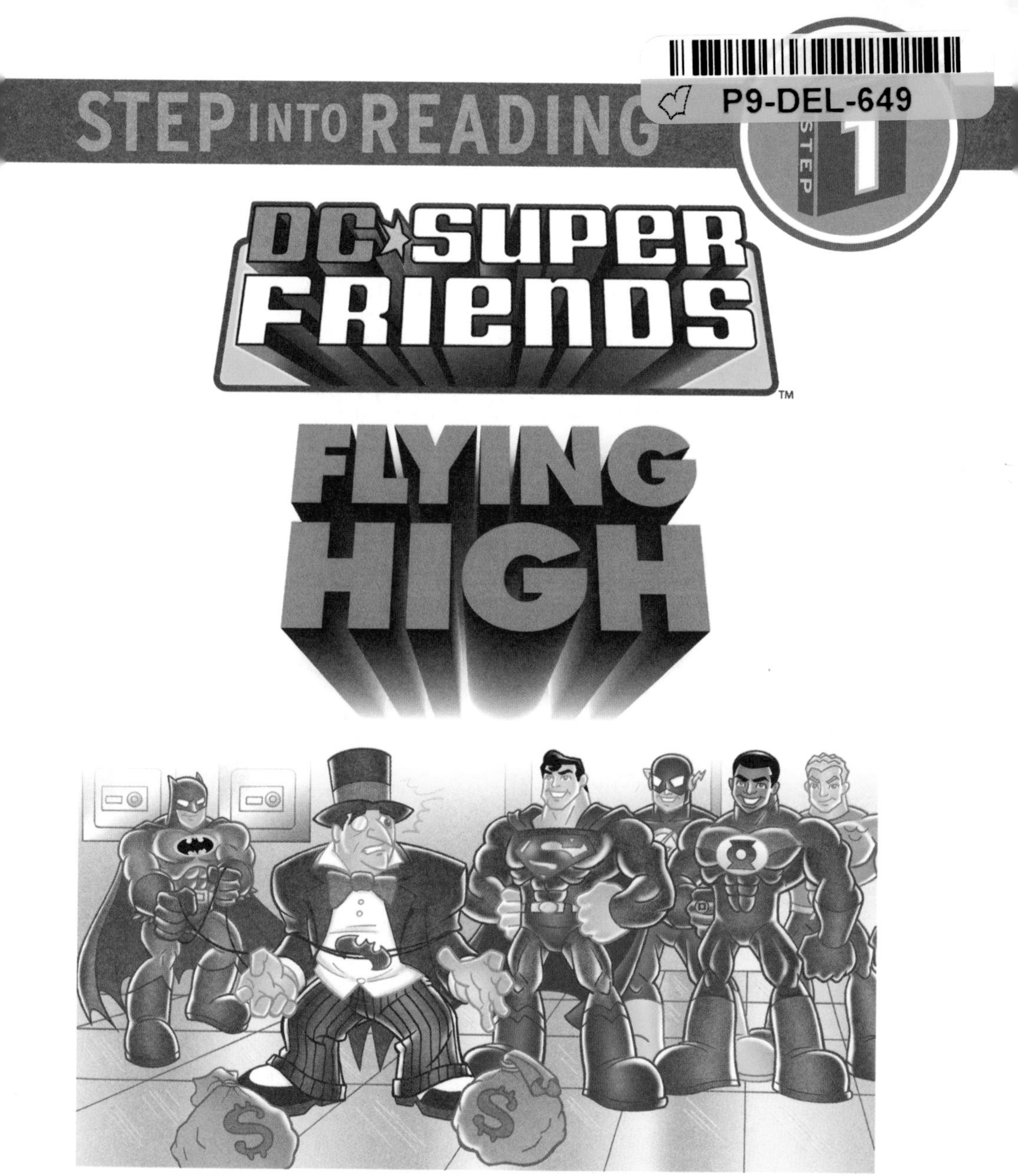

by Nick Eliopulos
illustrated by Loston Wallace and David Tanguay

Random House New York

Batman swings
over Gotham City.
The sun is shining.

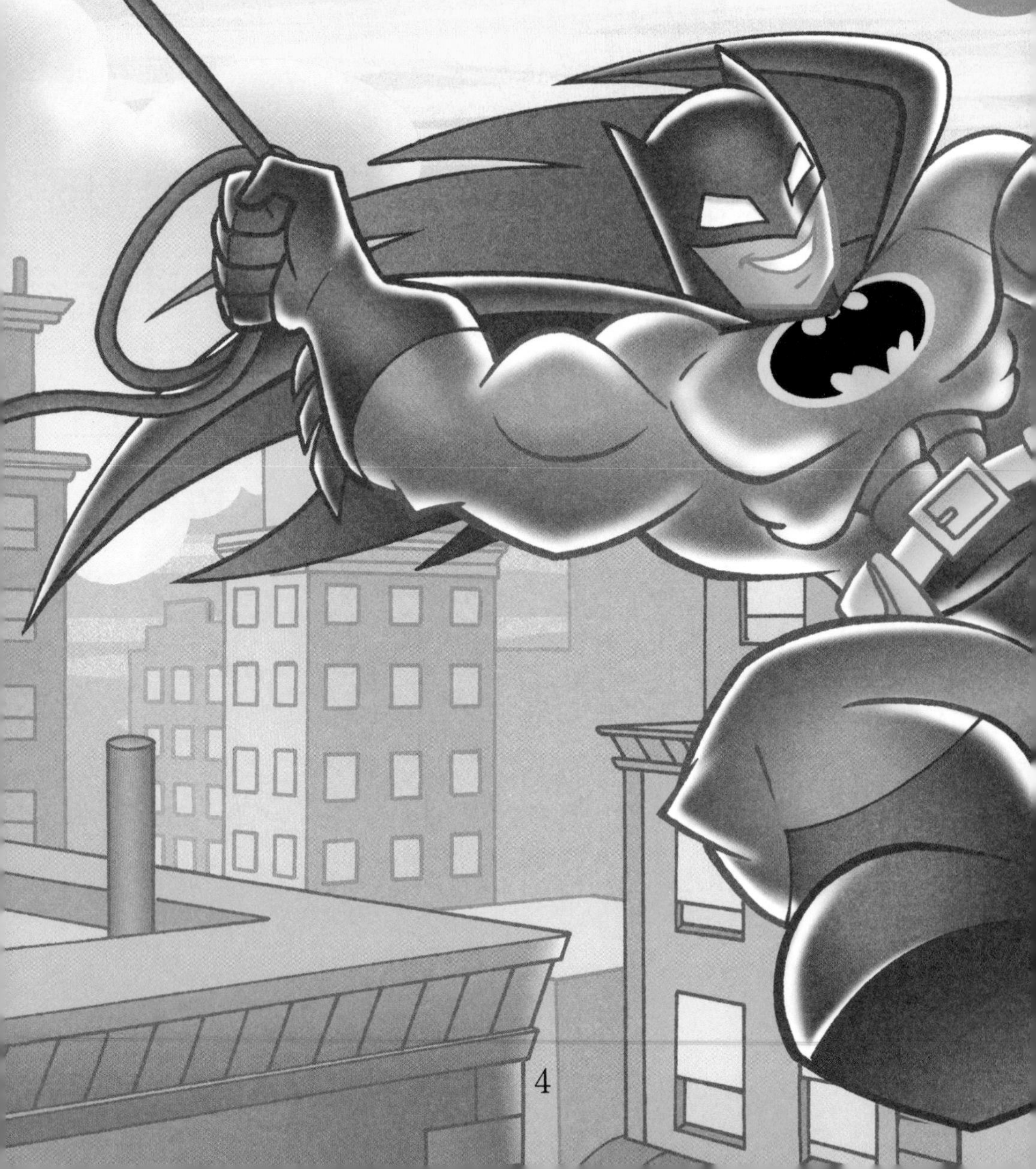

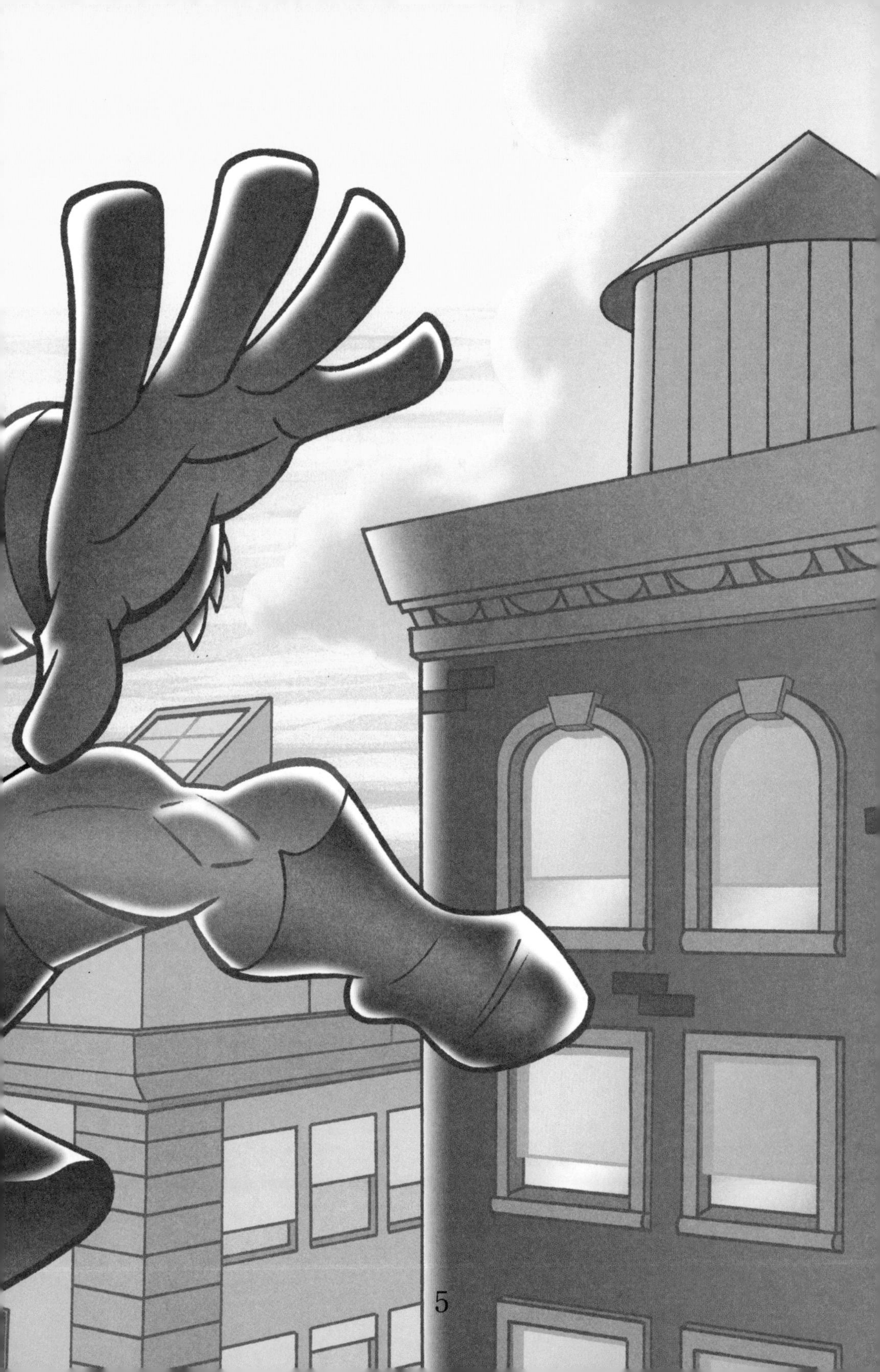

But something
strange is in the air.
The Super Friends
have work to do.

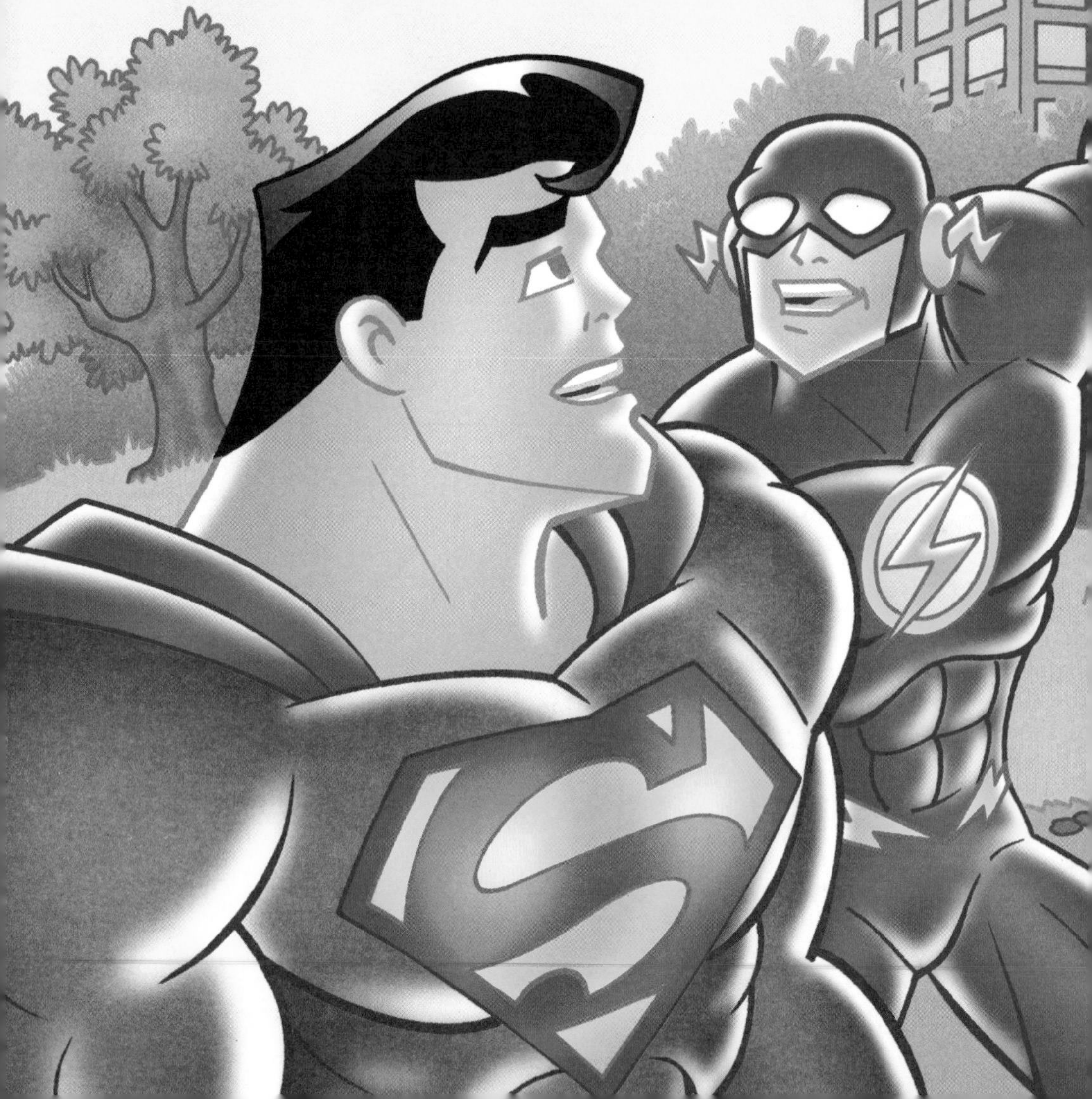

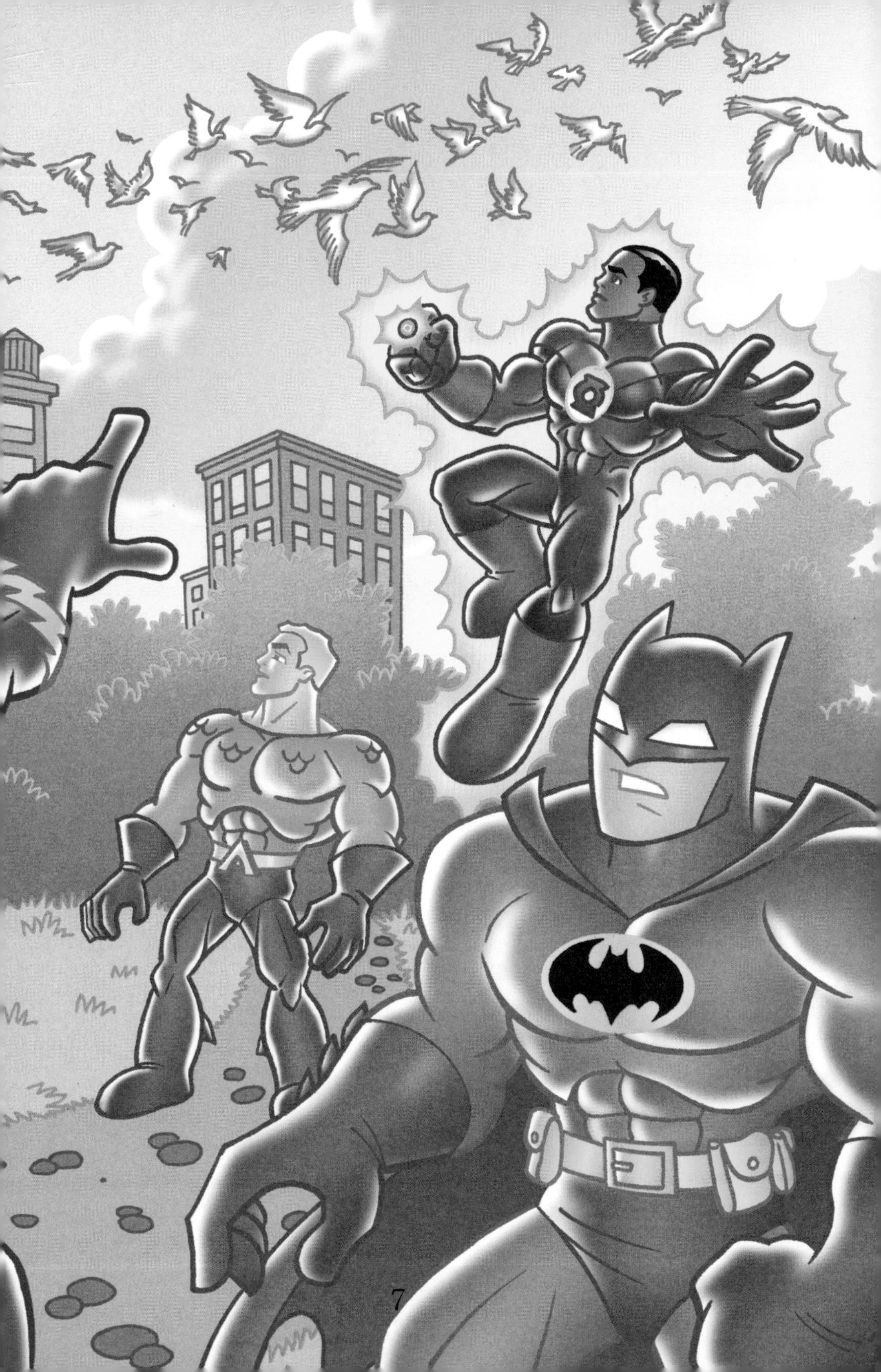

Honk! Honk!

Pigeons block traffic.

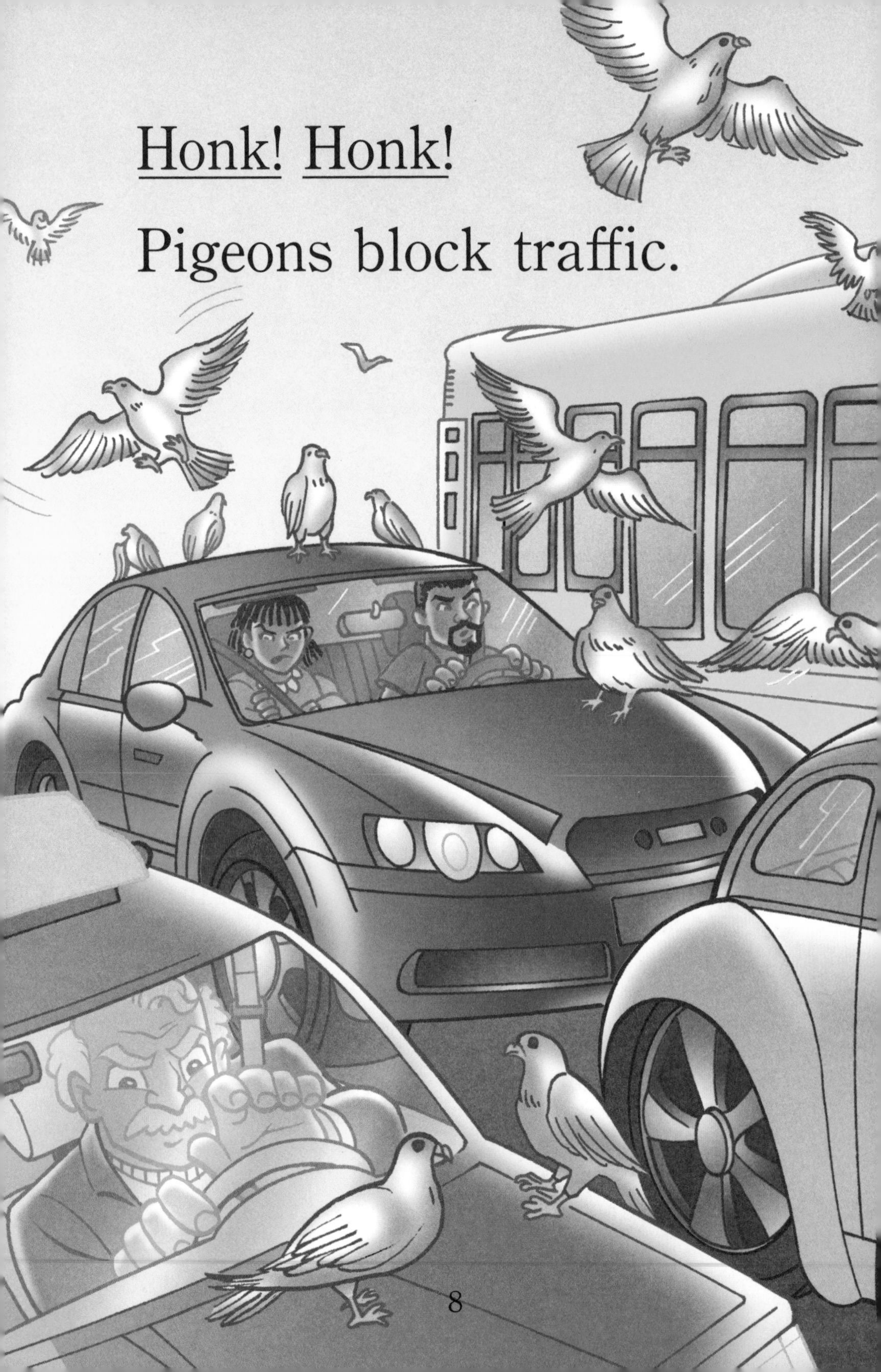

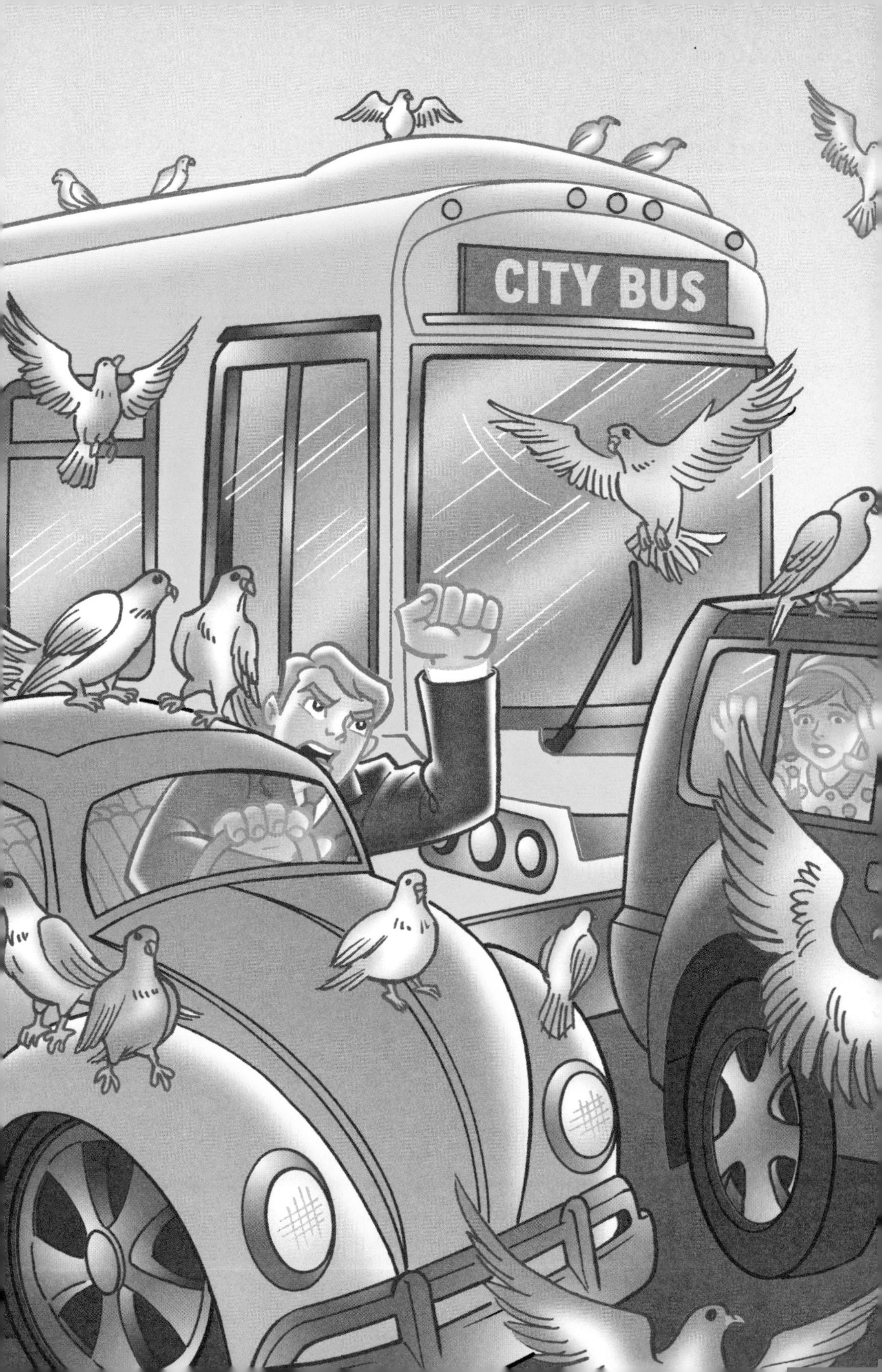
CITY BUS

Flash races

to the rescue!

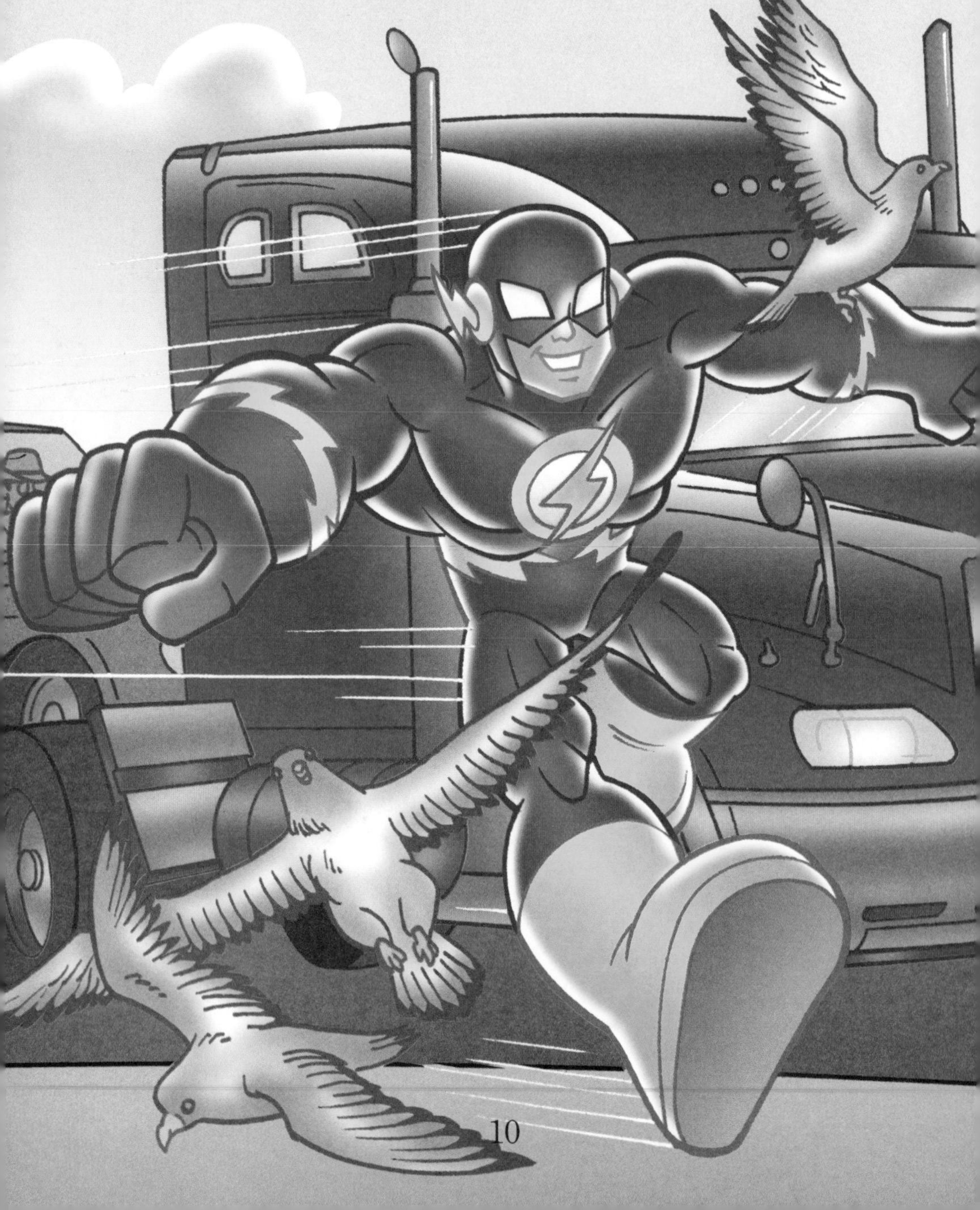

The pigeons

fly away.

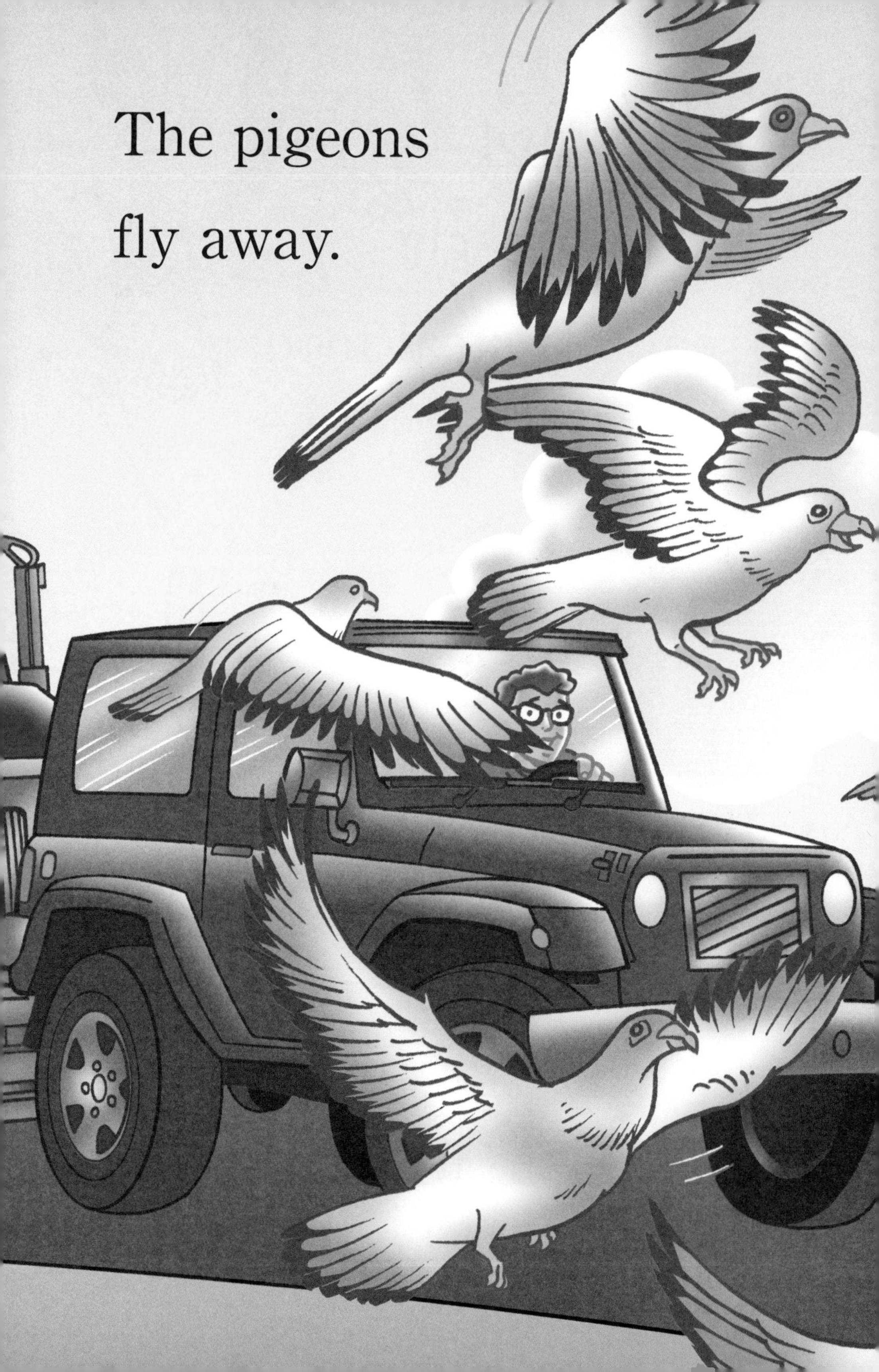

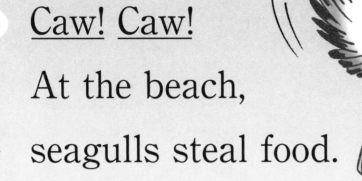

Caw! Caw!

At the beach,

seagulls steal food.

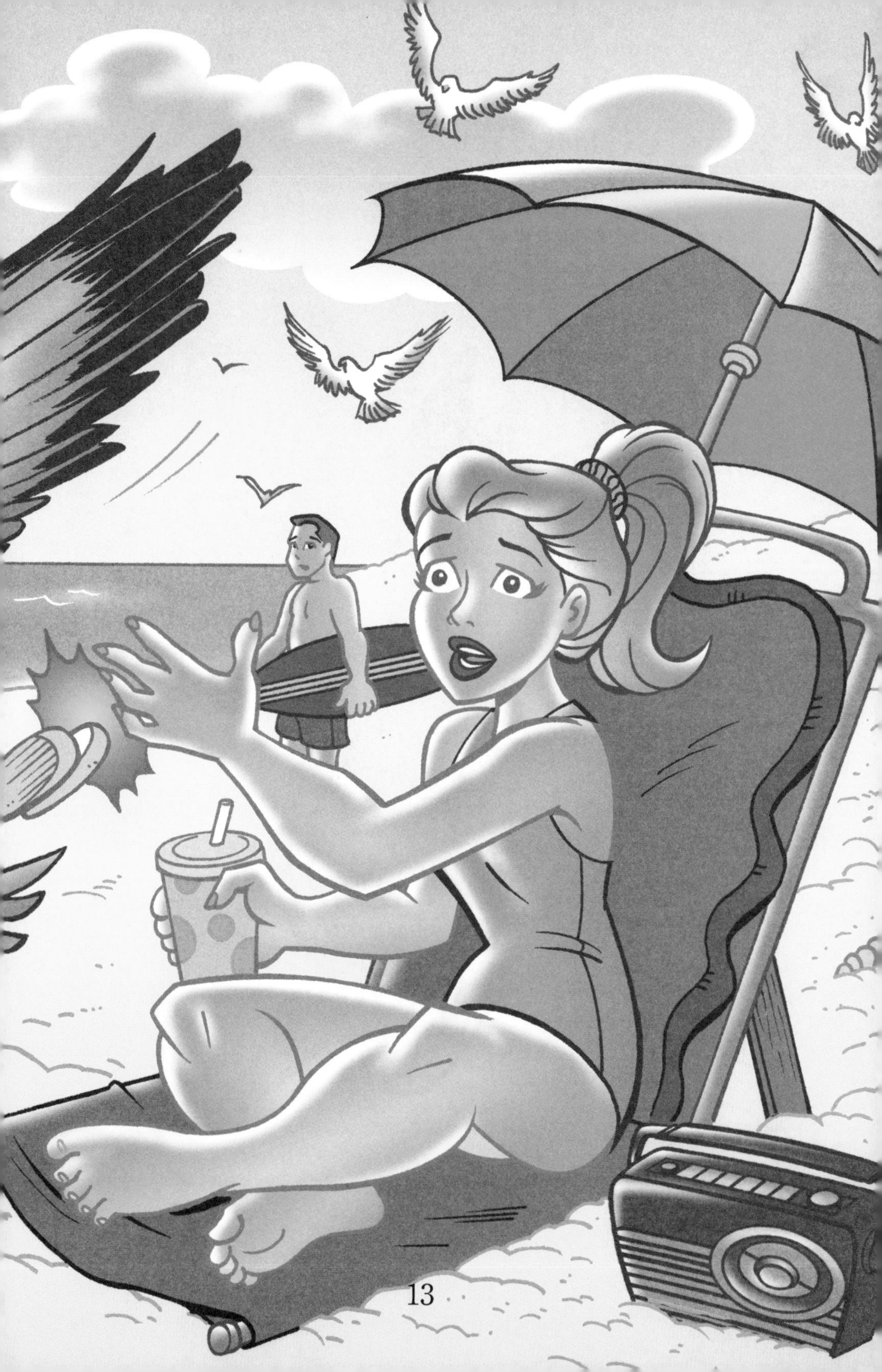

Aquaman

and his friend

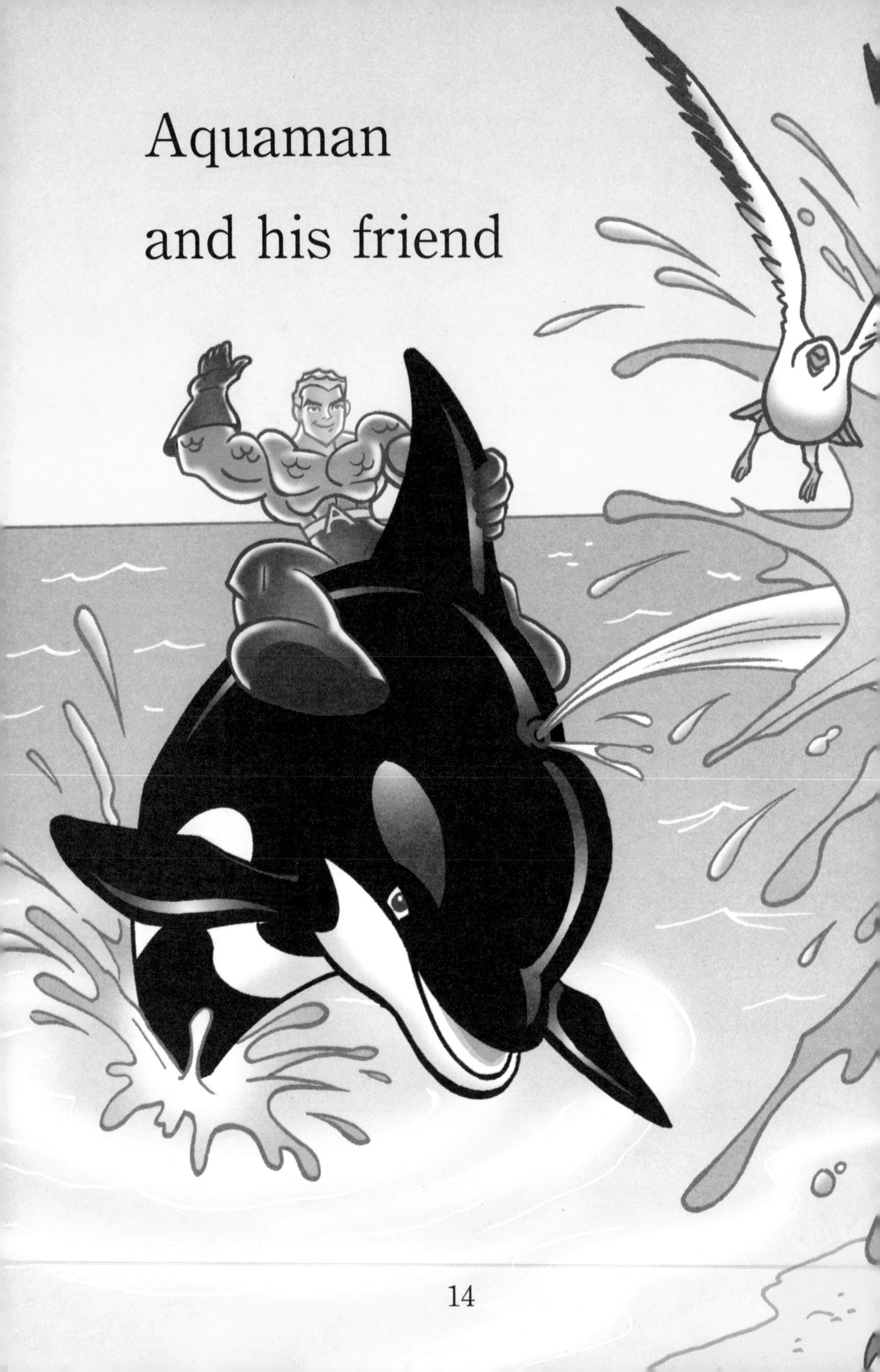

make a big splash!

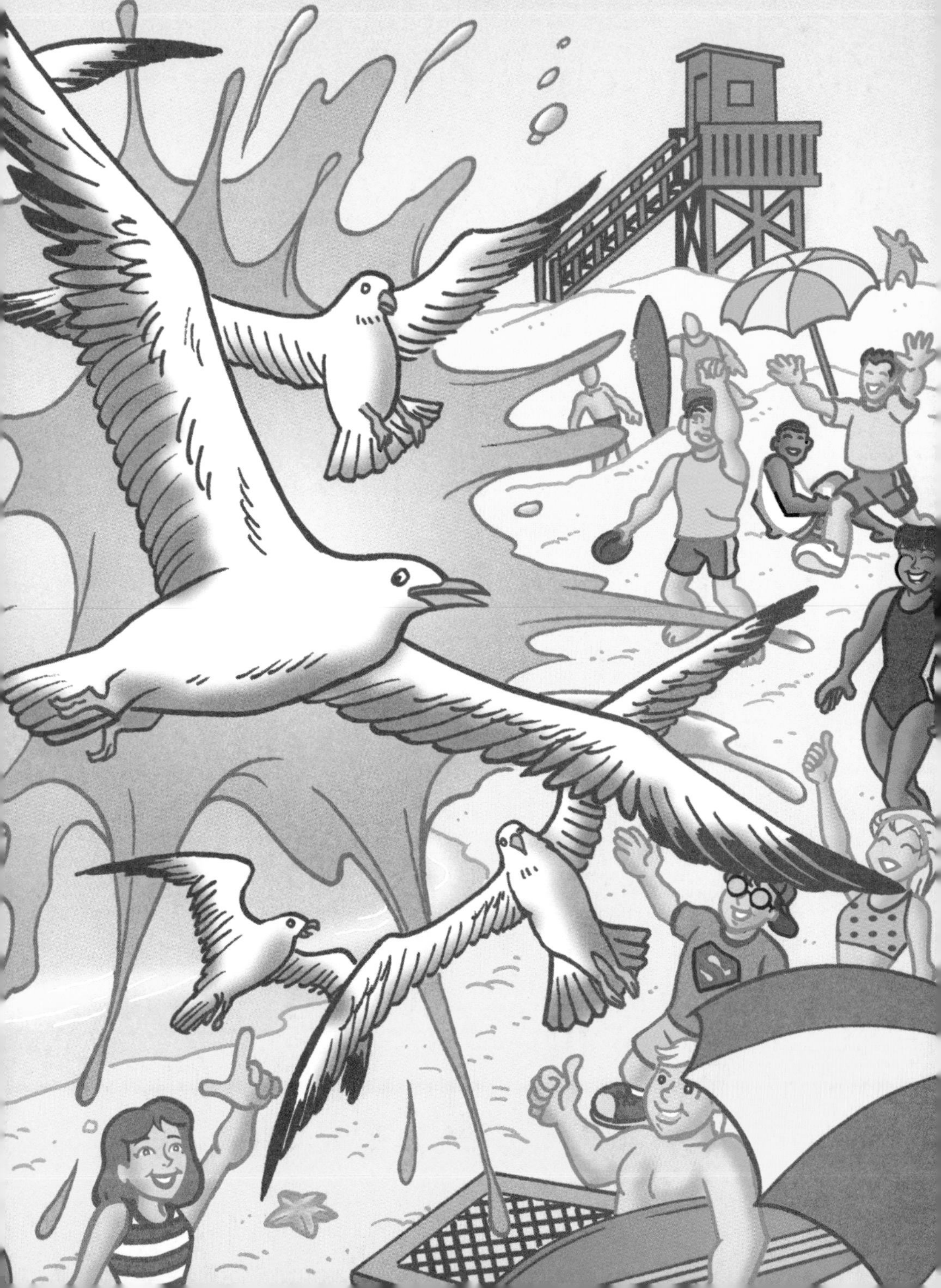

Squawk!

Ostriches run away

from the zoo.

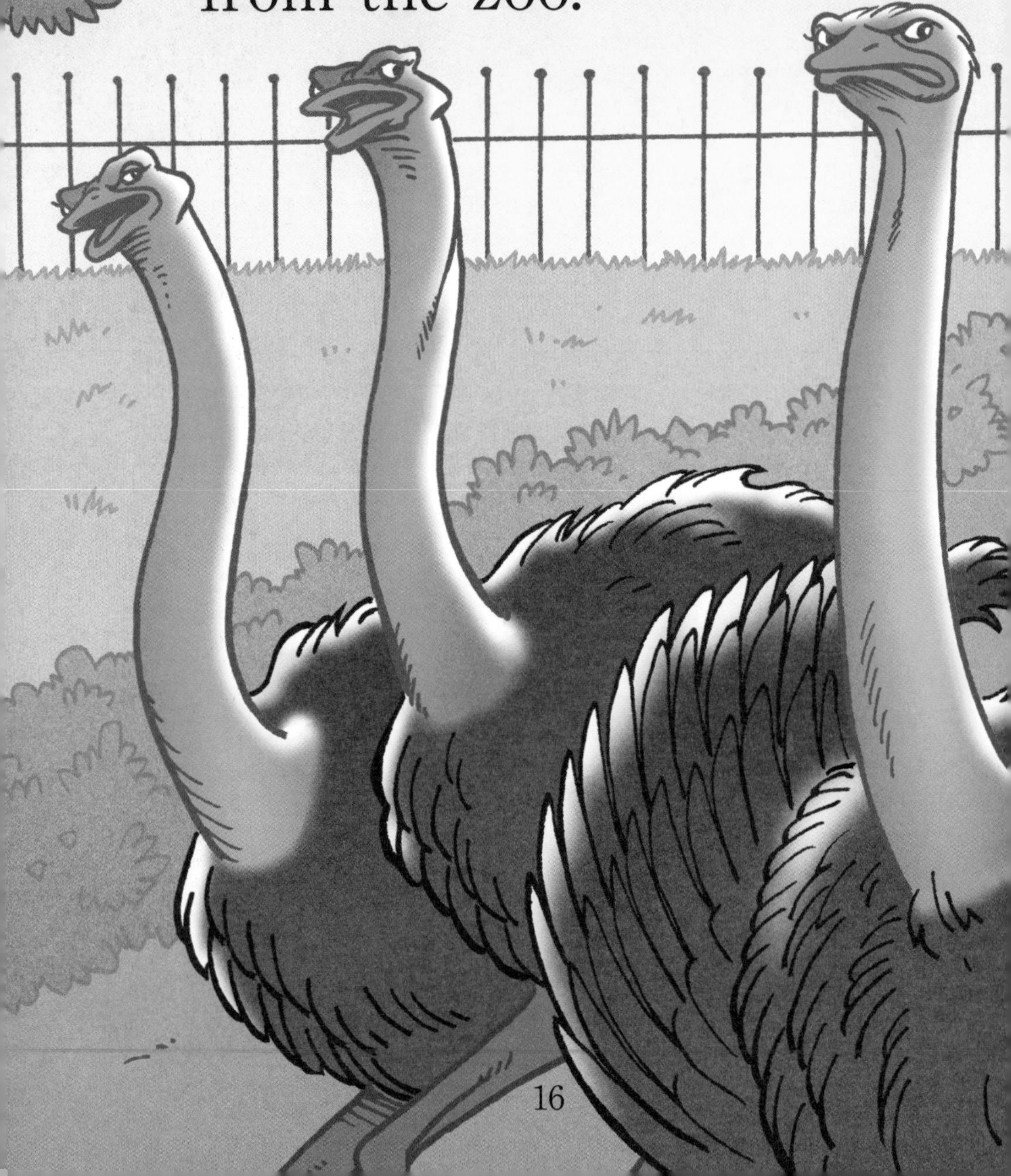

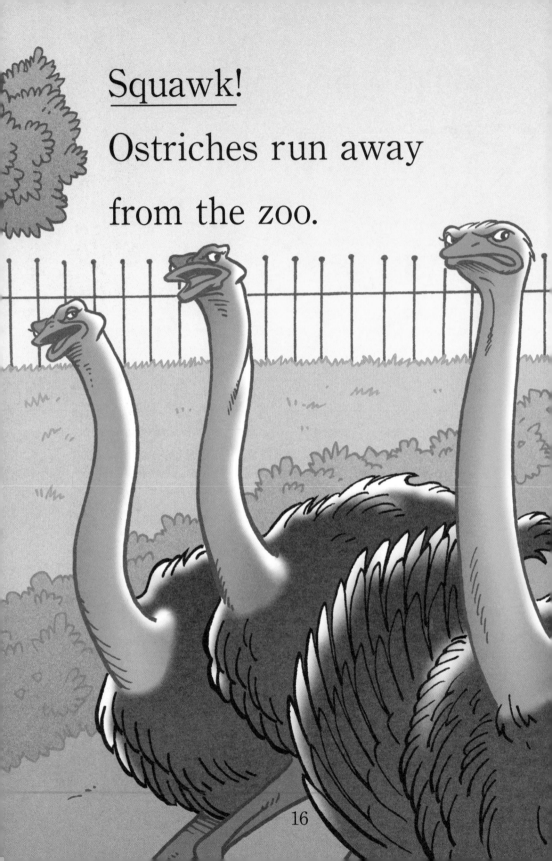

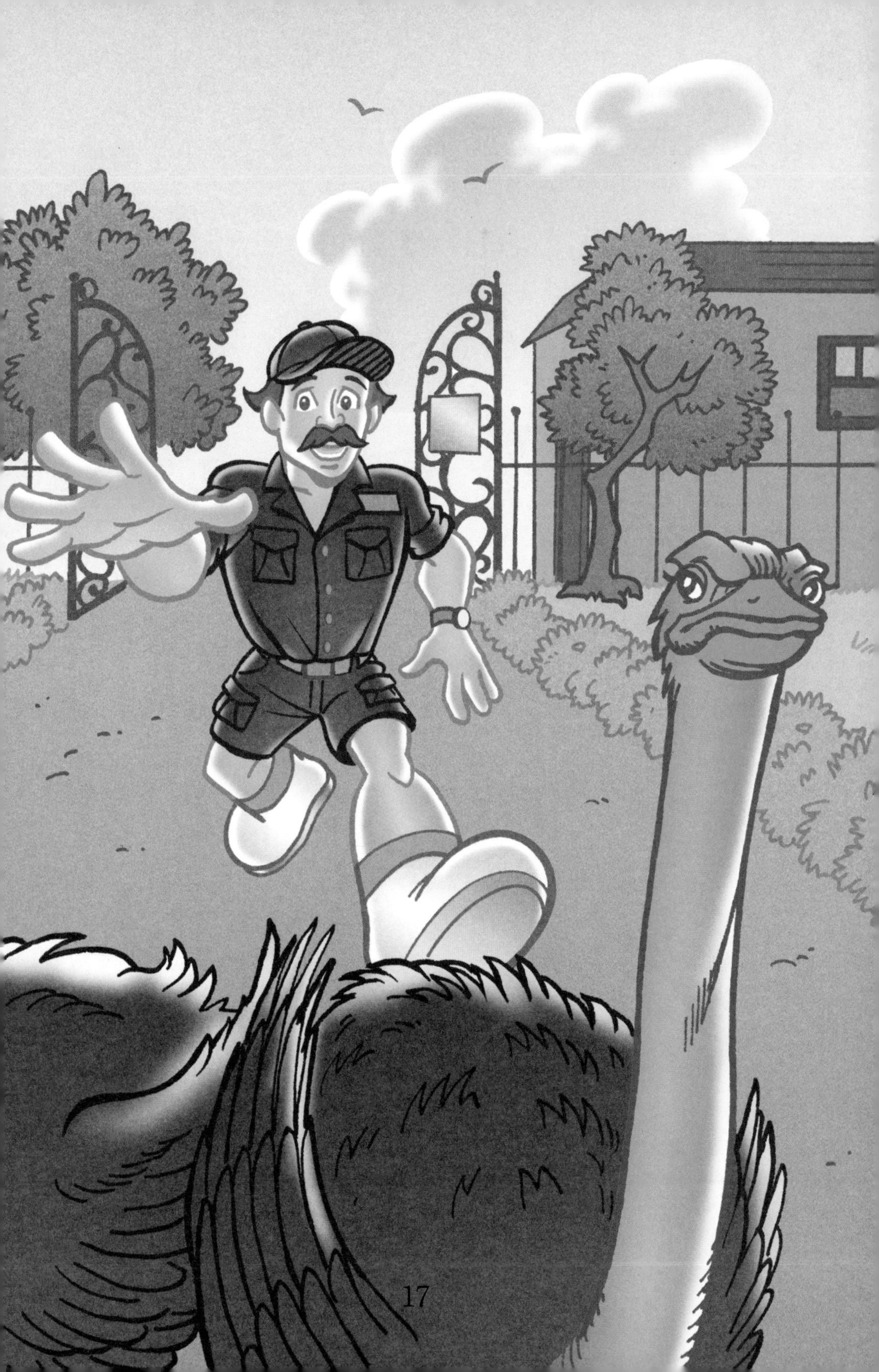

Superman and
Green Lantern
fly to the rescue!

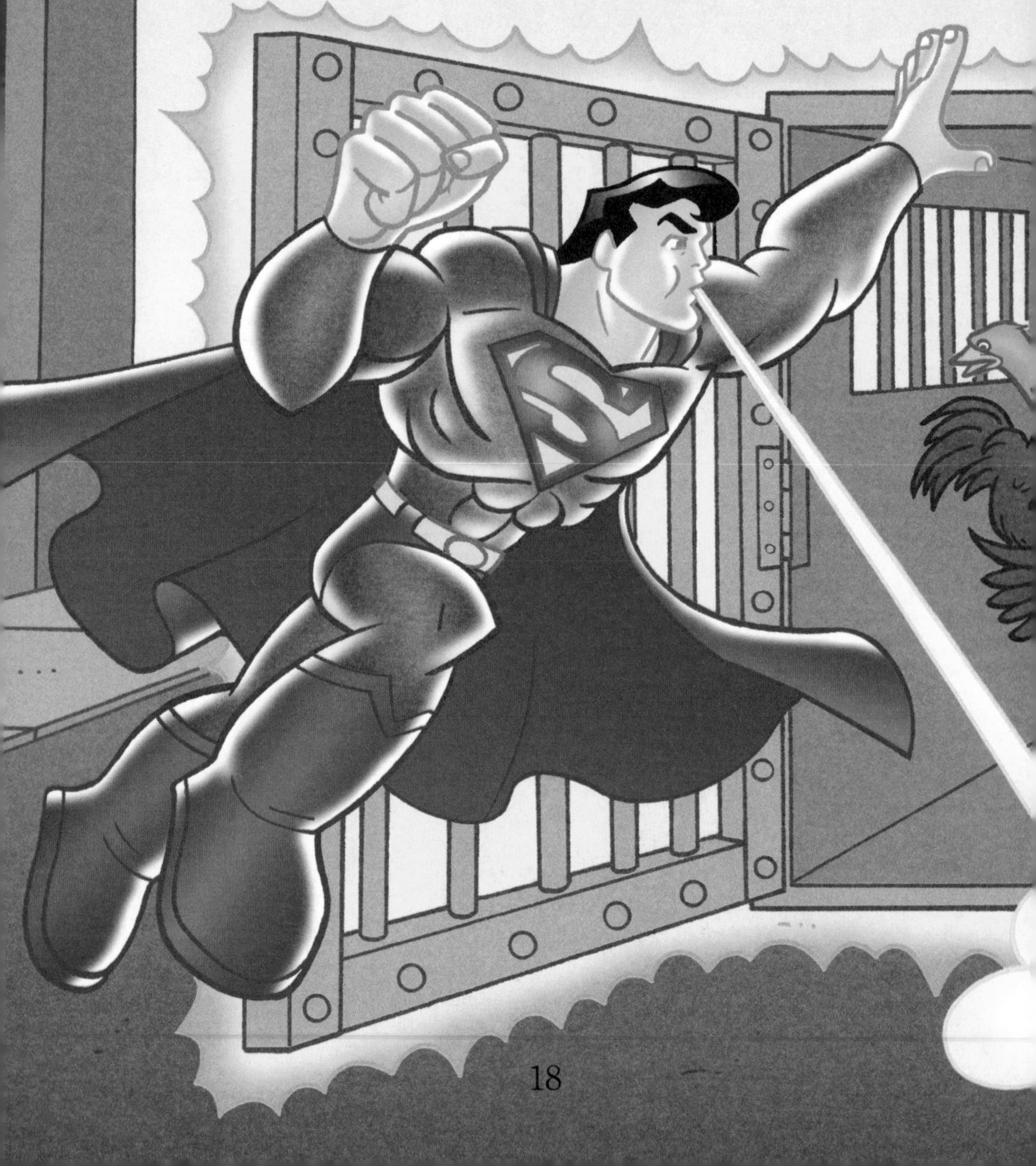

They stop the birds
in their tracks.

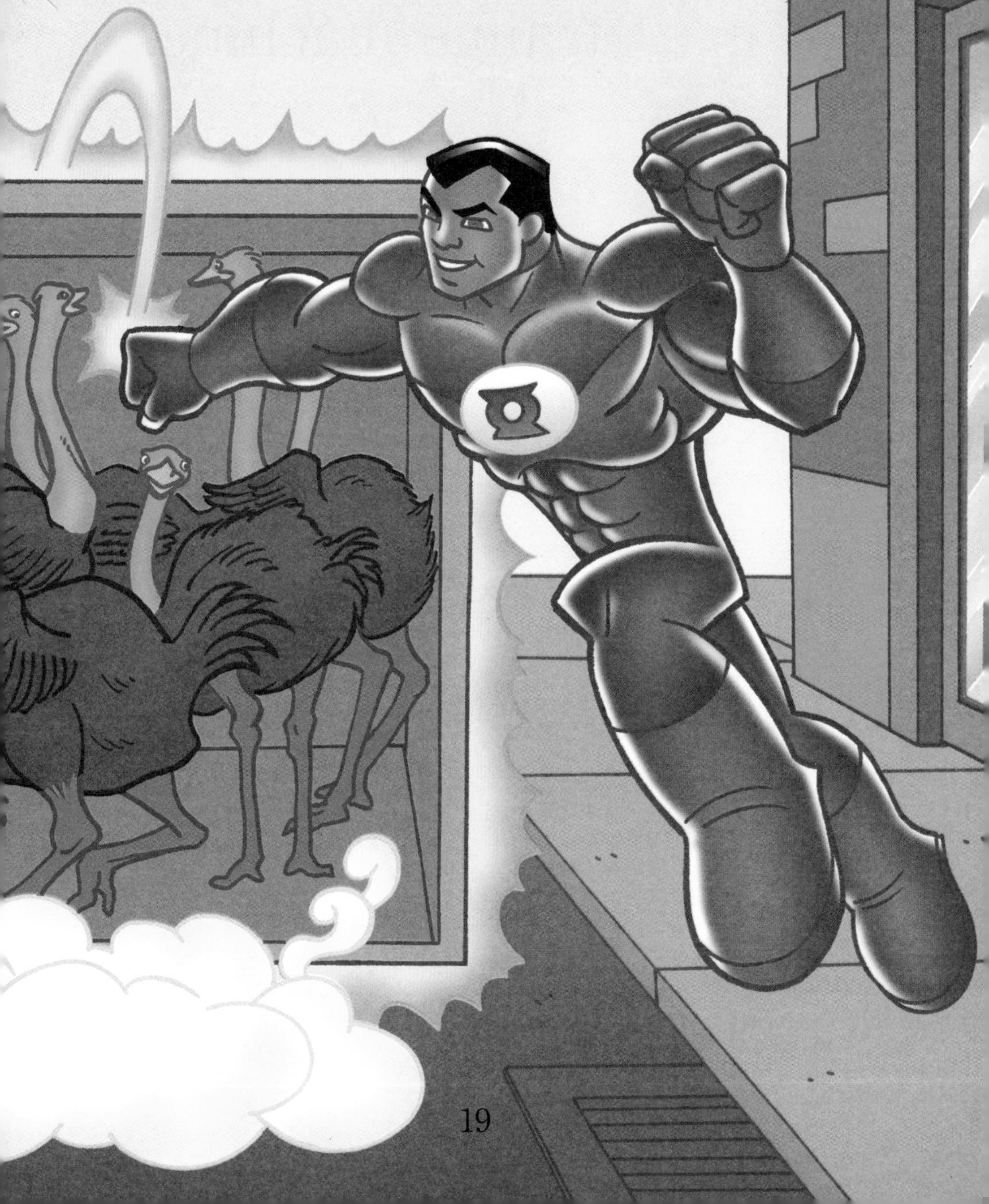

Hmmm.

Batman spots a clue.

It is a strange machine.

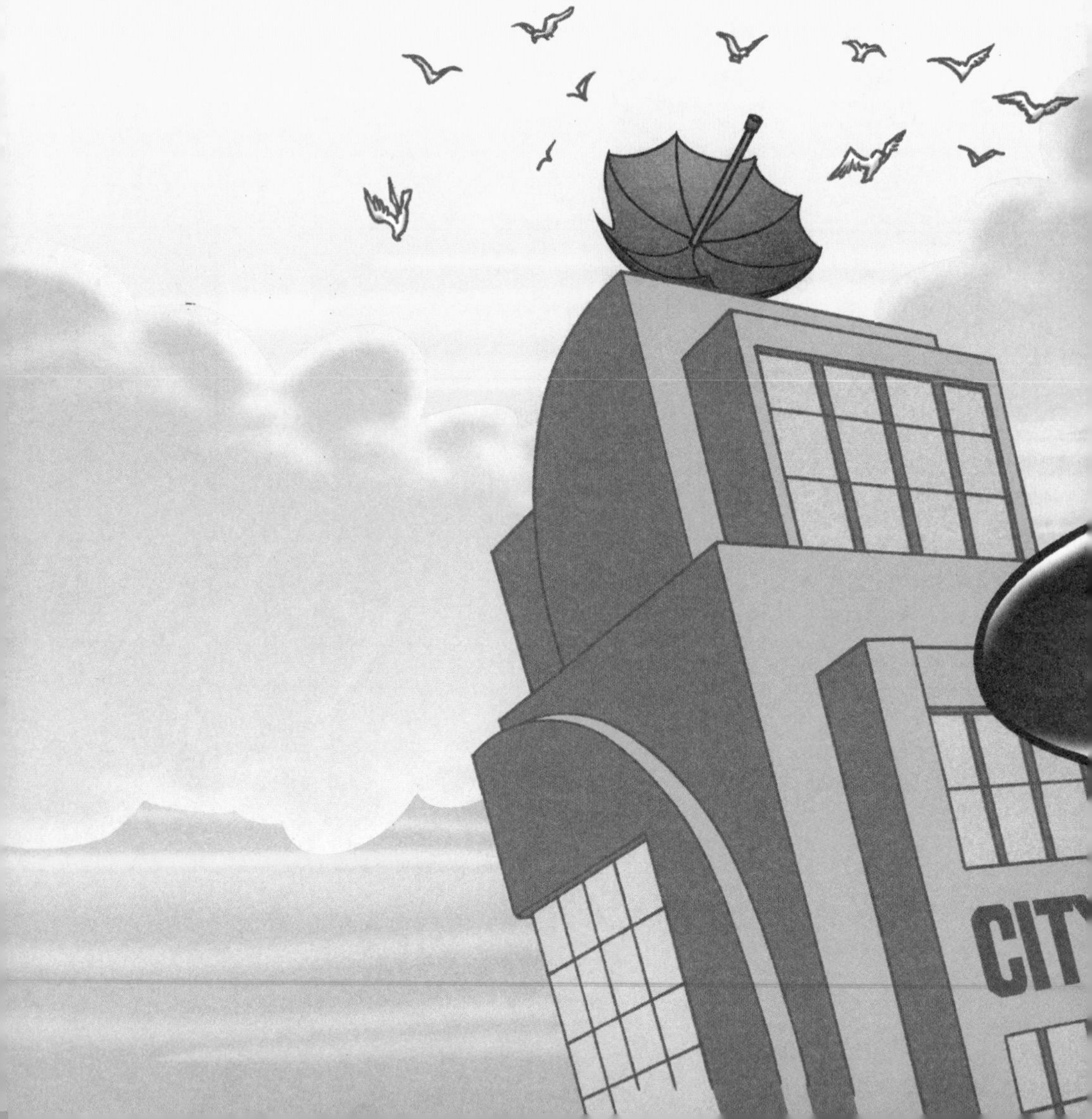

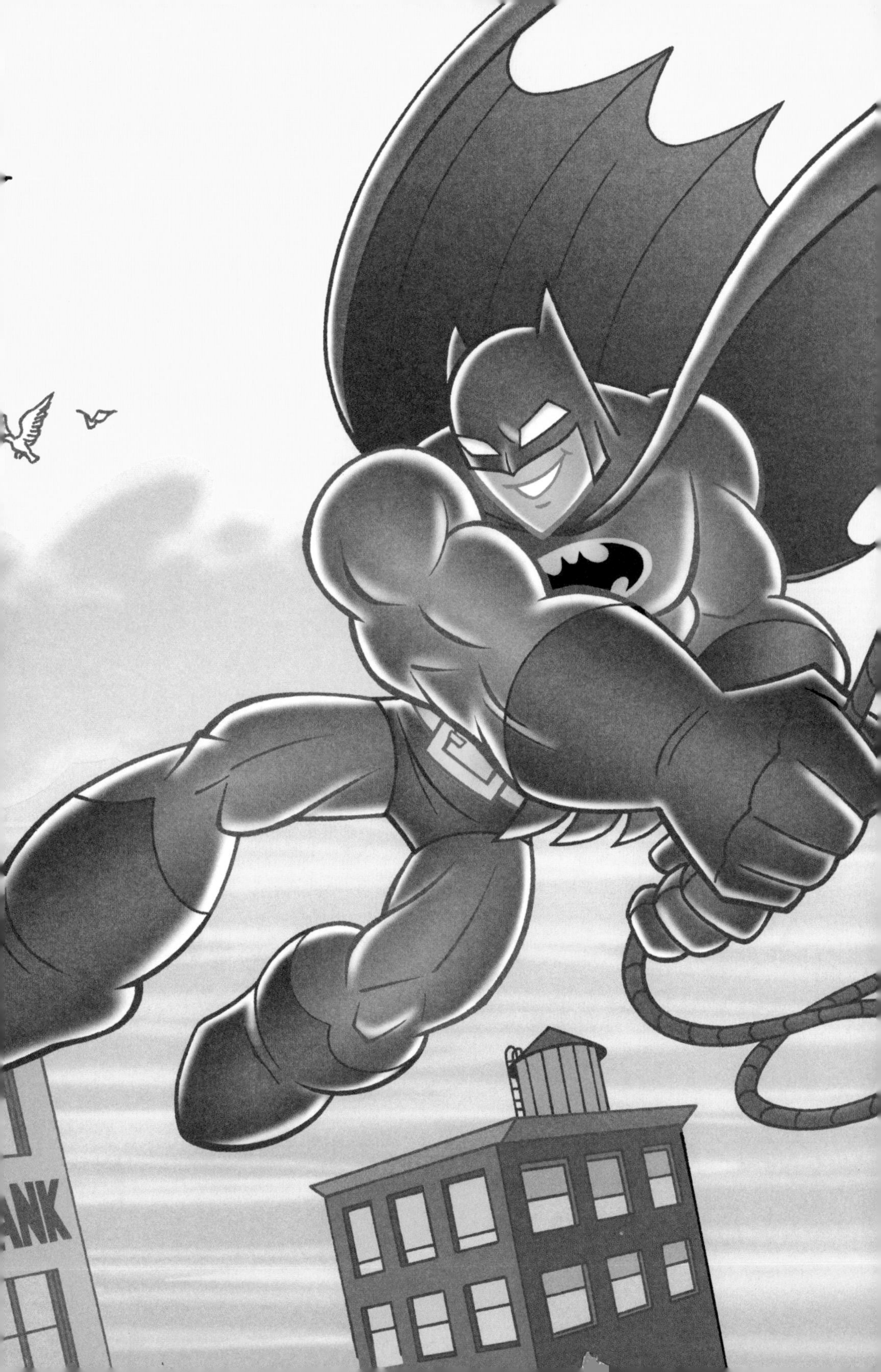
ANK

Batman takes
a closer look.
The noisy machine
bothers the birds.

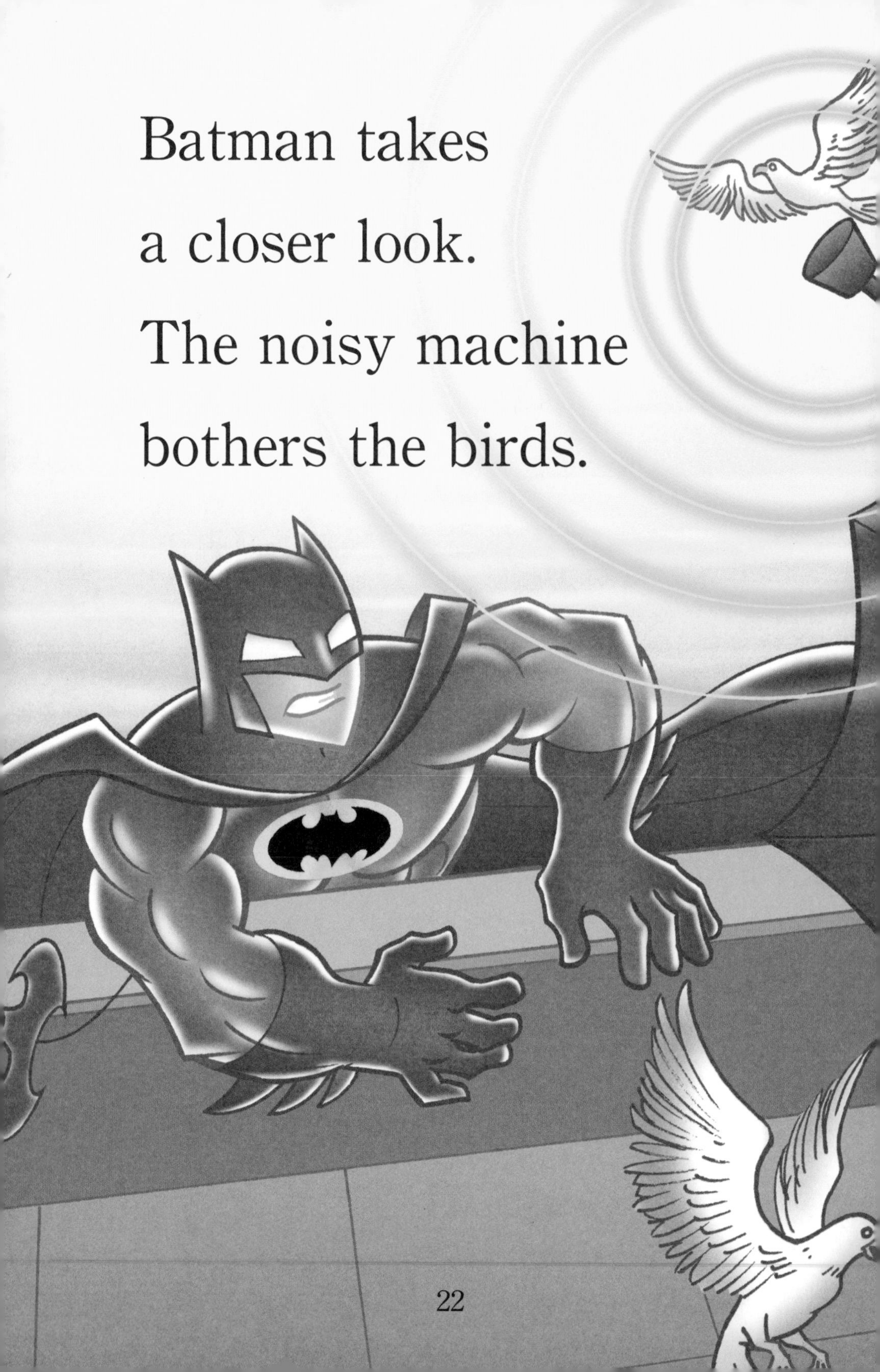

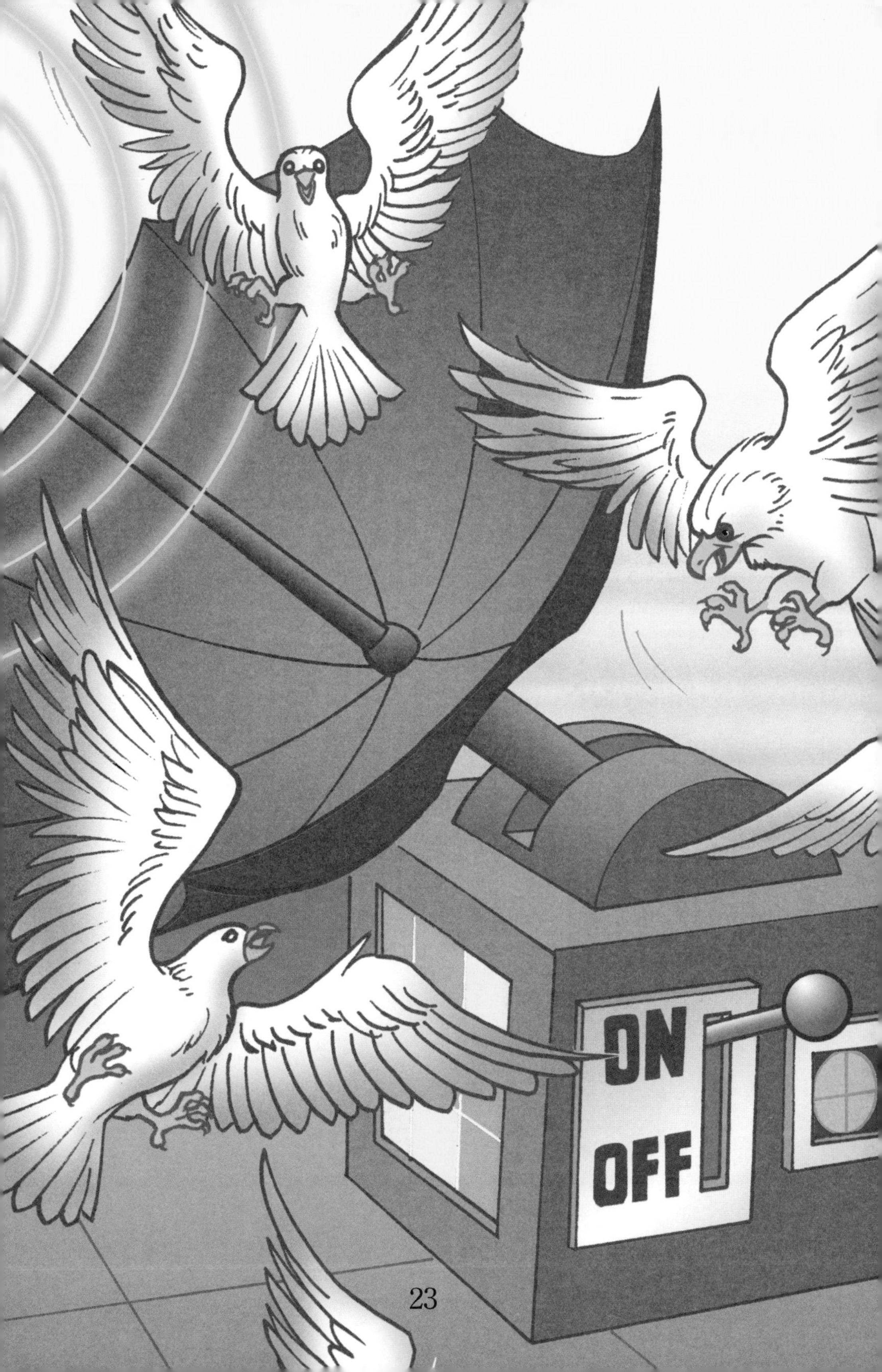
ON
OFF

Now the birds
are happy again.

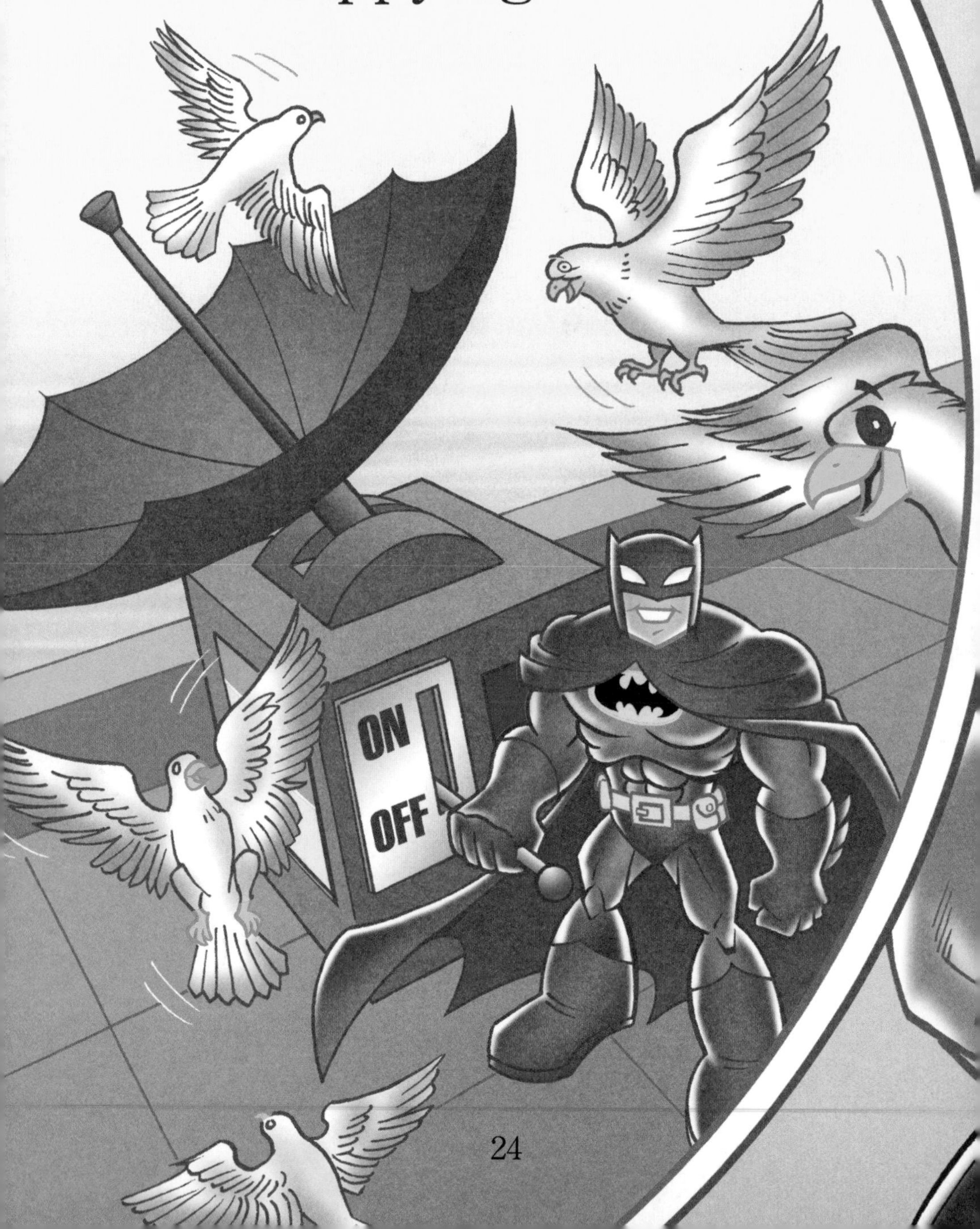
ON
OFF

Inside, the Penguin robs the bank.

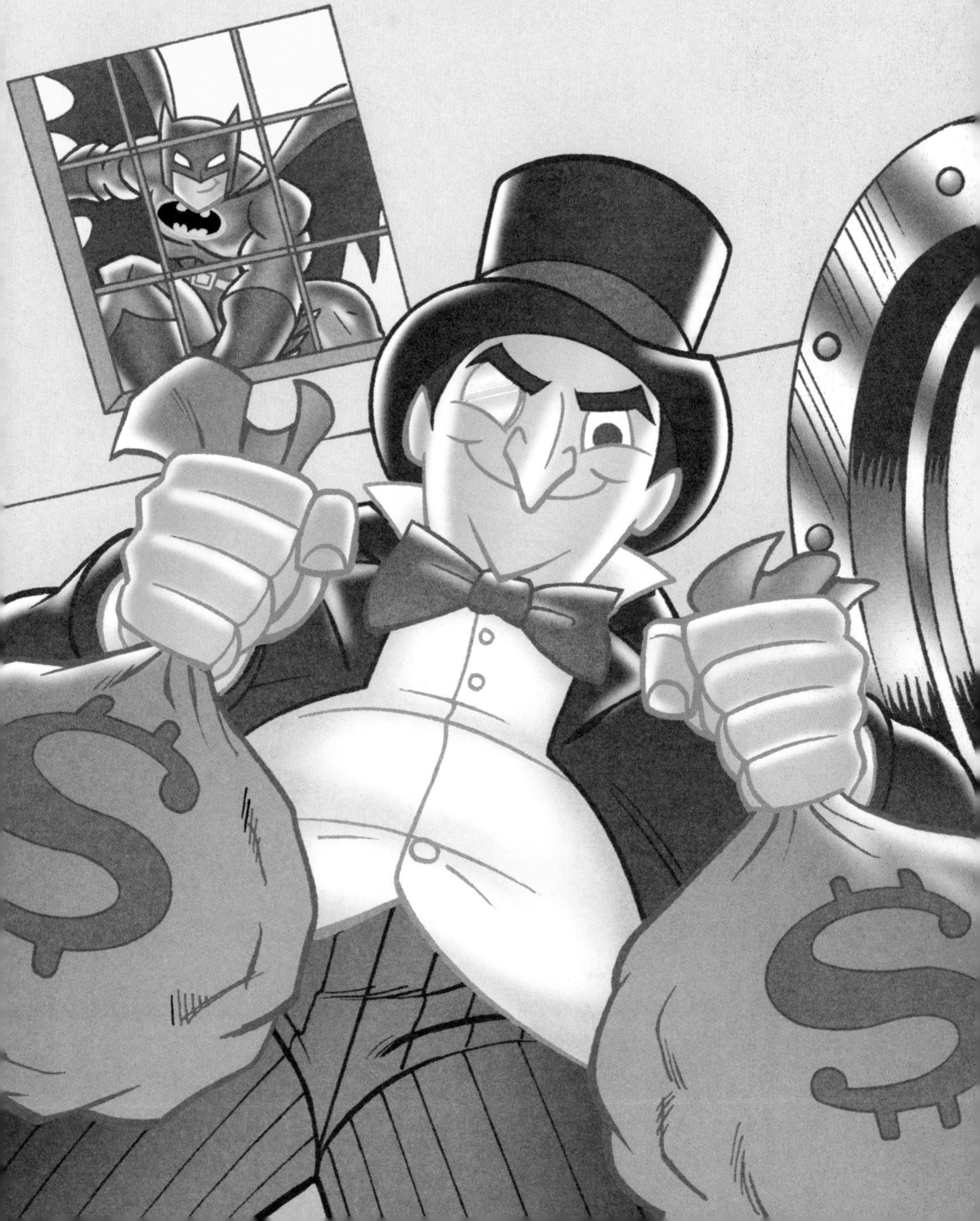

“The Super Friends
are too busy!
They can’t stop me,”
he says.

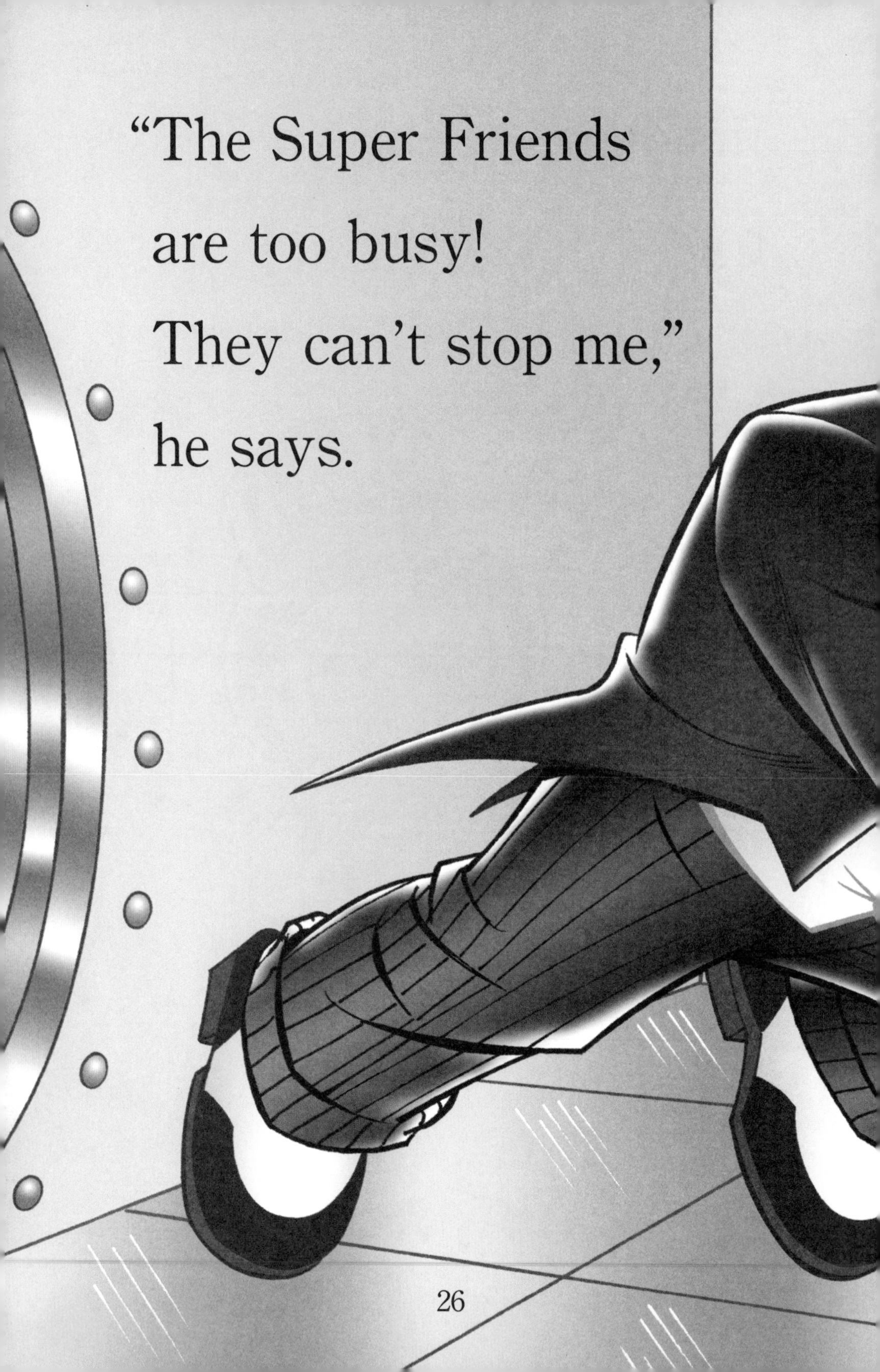

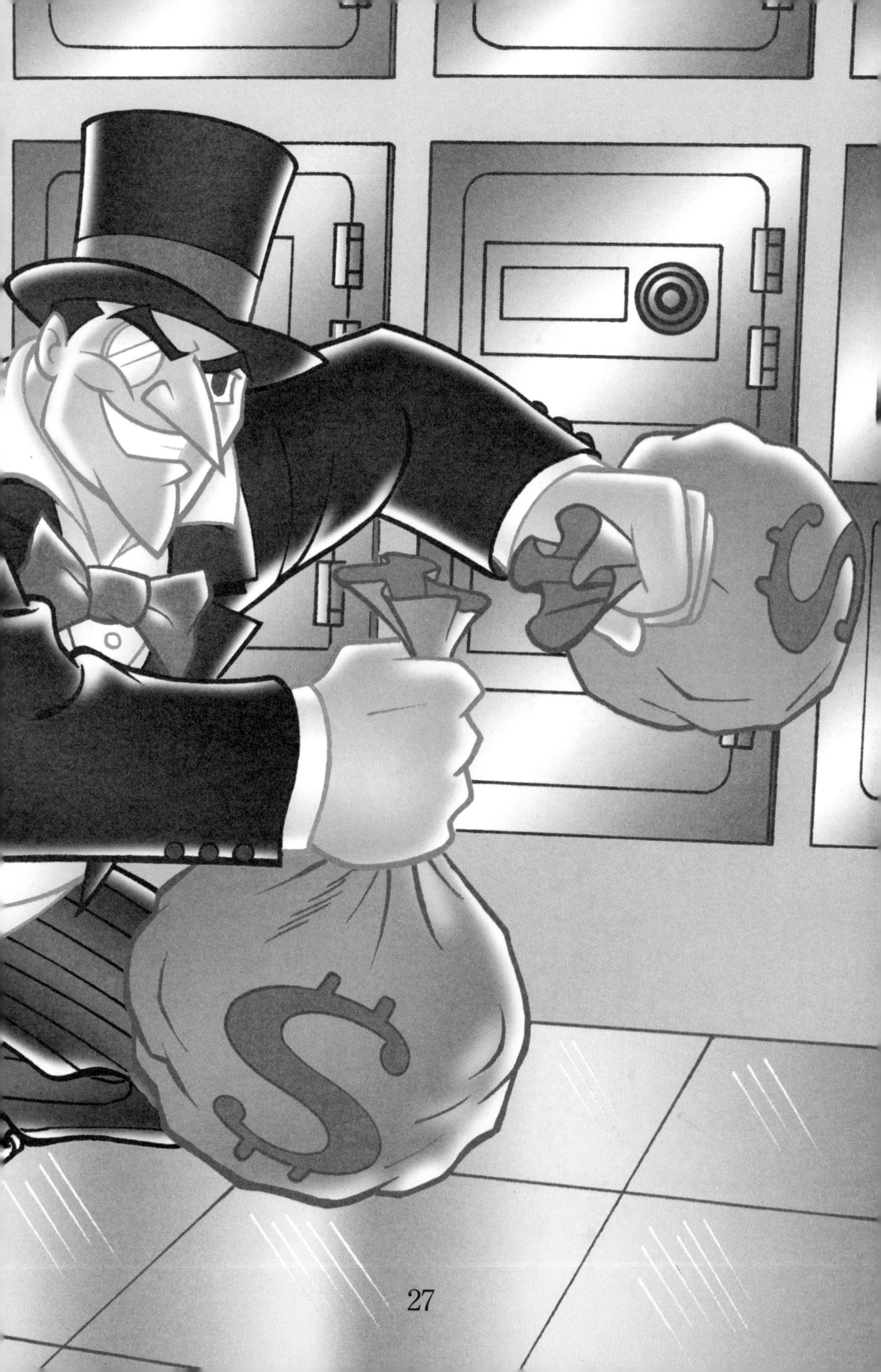

But Batman leaps

into action.

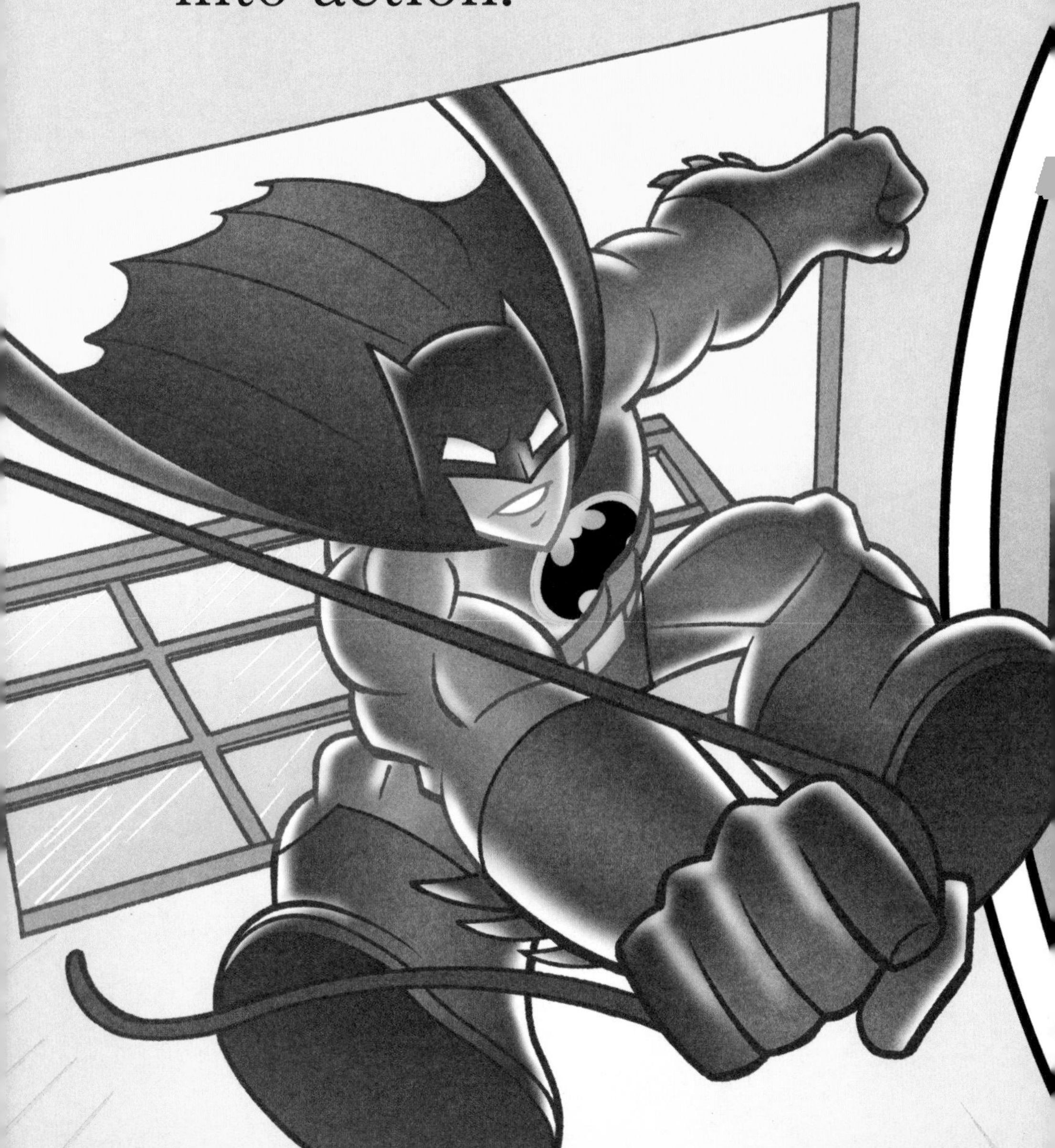

He stops

the Penguin's evil plan.

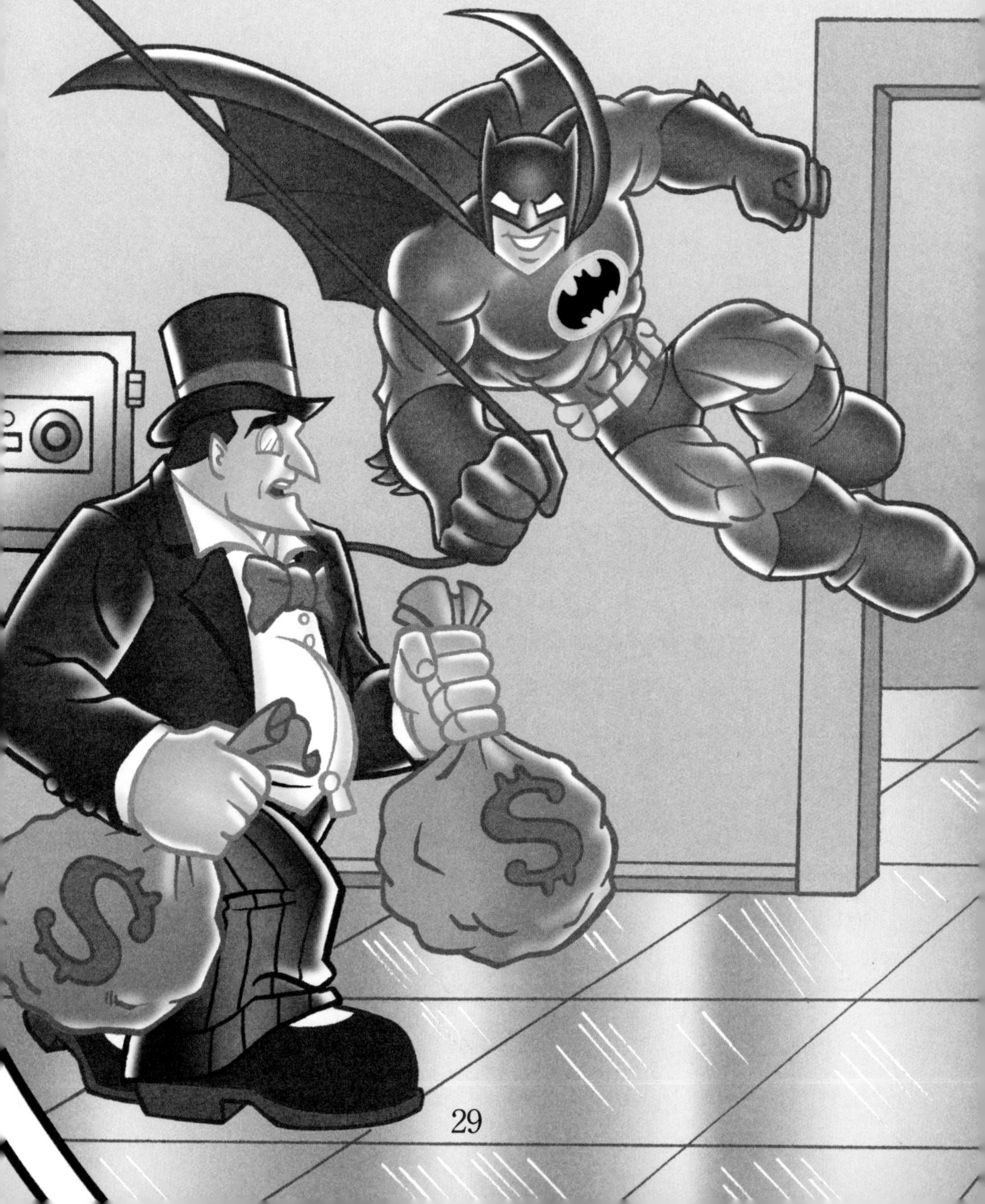

Teamwork

saves the day!

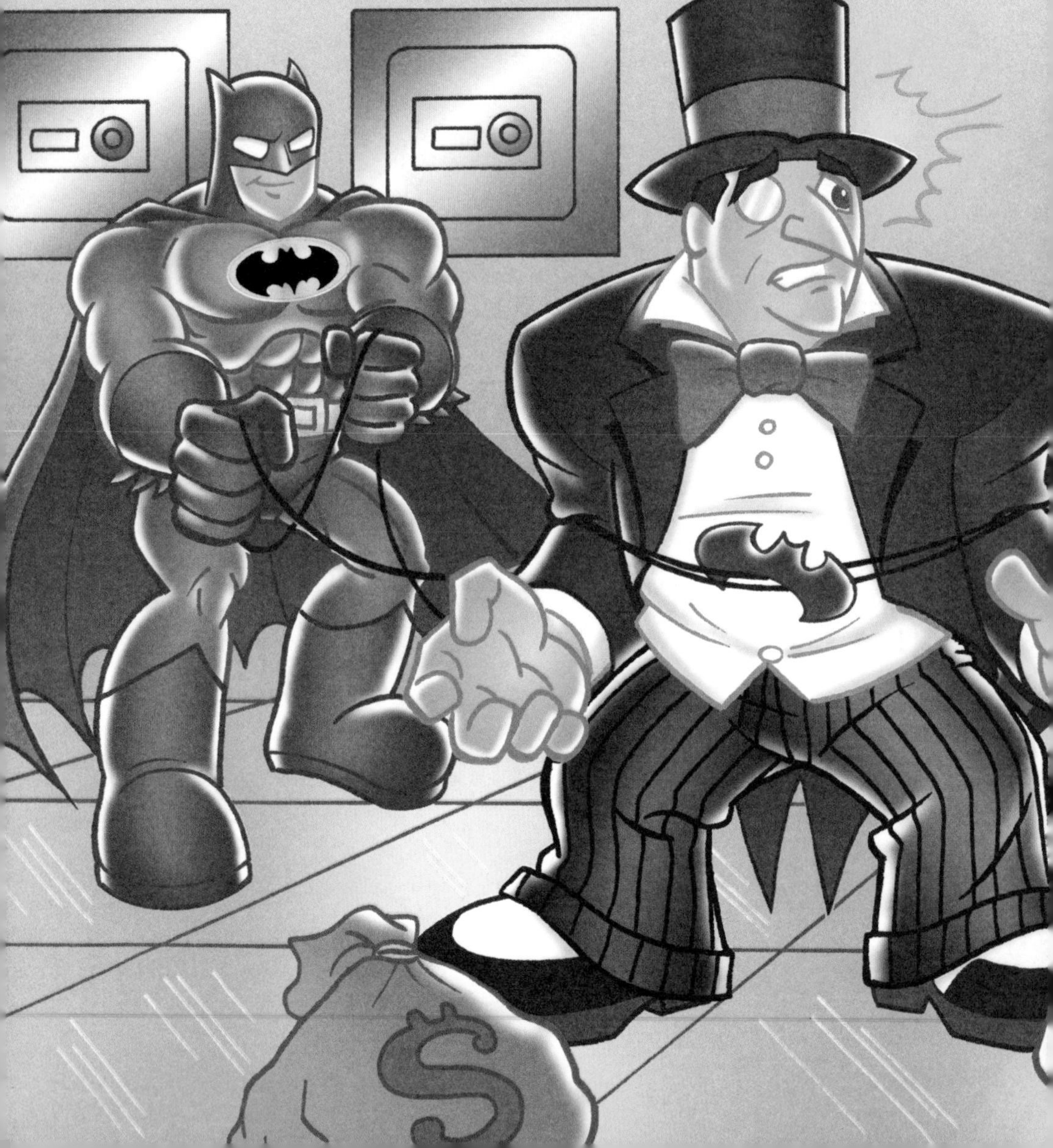

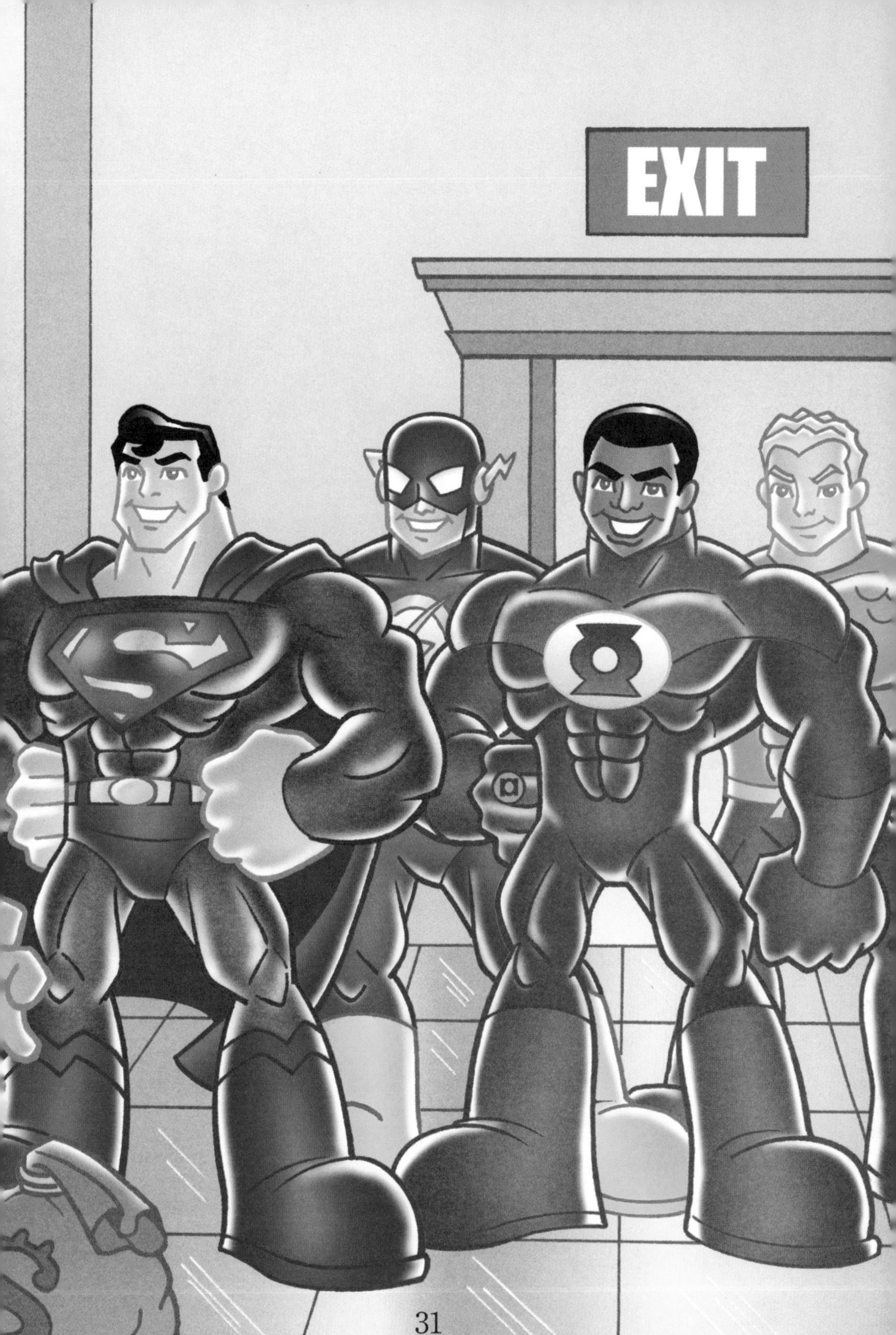
EXIT

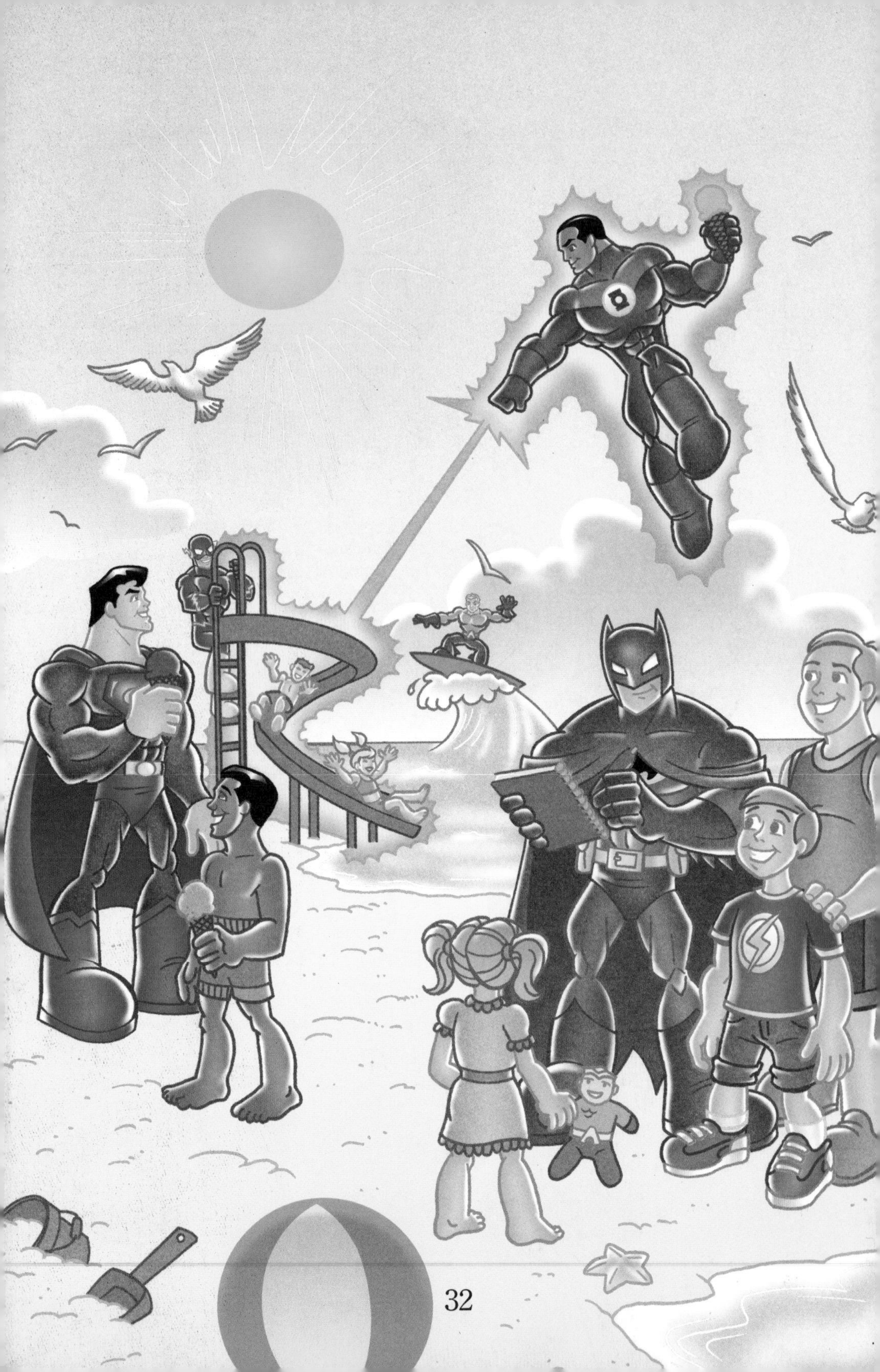